ALBERT

The Little Tree with Big Dreams

By Aaron and Will Eisenberg • Illustrated by Heather Martinez

 A GOLDEN BOOK • NEW YORK

No one loved Christmastime more than the plants at Earth Mama's nursery. Holiday cheer seeped through their roots. Maisie the palm tree swayed in her pot, and even Gene the stink-breath weed got in on the fun!

Little Albert was about to bring them more joy with a Christmas song.

"Who's ready to get their jingle on?" Albert called. "This is gonna be the Christmas-iest Christmas of all!"

But every year, as Albert watched all the big trees outside go home with happy families, he grew a little sad.

"Look at those guys," Albert sighed. "They're going to get shiny stars, and on Christmas morning, kids will go crazypants for the presents under their branches."

Albert loved his nursery family, but he knew he was destined for something greater. He hopped off his shelf and raced for the door.

Just then, Earth Mama, her son Donny, and her granddaughter Molly walked into the nursery. She spotted Albert on the floor.

"What in the world is this pip-squeak doing down here?" asked Earth Mama.

Molly placed Albert back on his shelf. "Don't feel bad," she whispered. "Lotsa people think I'm a pip-squeak, too. But it's okay to be small, as long as it doesn't stop you from doin' big things."

"Let's hit the road, Molly!" Donny called. "We've got a plant delivery at Baker's Hill before the Empire City Christmas show in New York."

Albert slumped in his pot . . . until a man on the TV caught his attention.

"Tomorrow in Baker's Hill, Vermont," the man explained, "one special tree, oozing with Christmas spirit, will be chosen as this year's Empire City Christmas Tree— the most famous Christmas tree in the world!"

A special tree, oozing with Christmas spirit? That sounded like Albert! He decided to do something big. He would sneak a ride to Baker's Hill with the girl and her dad.

Gene thought Albert was out of his mulch.

But Maisie believed in him. She wanted to come along!

The second the coast was clear, Albert and his buddies snuck out to Donny's truck to stow away in the back. Maisie bent her trunk backward and launched Albert and Gene into the truck, then jumped in behind them. They waved goodbye to their Earth Mama's family and set off.

Soon Molly and Donny stopped for lunch at a restaurant called Cactus Pete's.

"Help!" a voice called from beneath the snow. Albert got out of the truck and started digging. He was surprised to find Cactus Pete himself!

The freezing cactus groaned. "E-e-every winter I'm tossed out so some s-s-stinkin' Christmas tree can take my place inside."

Maisie perked up. "Did you say Christmas tree? Albert here is going to be the Empire City Christmas Tree!"

"Oh, *is he?*" sneered Pete, sharpening his needles.

"Well, considerin' I *hate* Christmas," he howled, "allow Cactus Pete to show y'all a prickly good time!"

Pete and his ragtag band of cacti chased after Albert, Maisie, and Gene, blasting spiky needles in every direction! Many of Albert's ornaments fell to the ground and shattered.

But Albert and his friends bested the cacti and rolled a dumpster right at Cactus Pete, flattening him like a pancake.

Albert, Maisie, and Gene headed back to Donny's truck, but discovered it was gone!

"Here's an idea," Gene suggested hopefully. "Let's all just go back to Earth Mama's and live merrily ever after!"

"We can't quit now," Albert protested.

Just then, another truck passed. BAKER'S HILL was painted in big letters on the side. Albert, Maisie, and Gene jumped aboard.

But later, when the truck dumped them onto a conveyor belt, the trio realized that something was wrong. This wasn't Baker's Hill—it was Baker's *Mill*! The plants lurched toward a treacherous tree-mulching machine. They were about to become paper!

Worse yet, Cactus Pete had survived the dumpster smash and followed them! He started firing spikes at Albert like daggers!

"Fa-la-la-la-losers!" Pete snarled.

Before the cactus could do any more damage, he rolled straight into the chipper.

Maisie shut her eyes in fear. She and Albert were next!

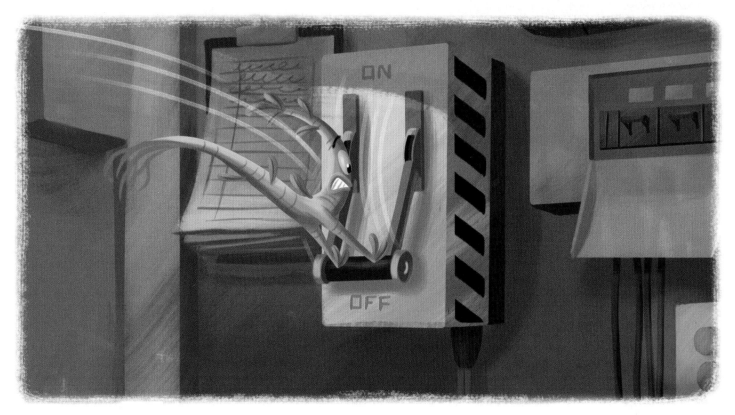

At the very last second, Gene used all his might to pull the emergency OFF lever. He saved his buddies!

Albert and his friends hopped to safety, but their journey was far from over.

The plants escaped and headed into a nearby forest in search of Baker's Hill. There they came across a family of rabbits.
"Aww! Fuzzy widdle bunnies!" Maisie gushed. *CHOMP!*
A rabbit took a giant bite out of her leaves.
"It's a vegetarian!" yelled Gene. "Run!"

They all jumped onto a log and slid down an enormous hill.

The plants skidded to a stop right in front of a news van. There was the man Albert had seen on TV!

Albert knew that this wasn't just any hill. It was Baker's Hill! They'd made it to the tree selection right on time!

During the long and bumpy trip, all but one of Albert's ornaments had broken. But Maisie gave him a Christmas makeover, tidying him up and dusting him with a fresh coat of snow.

"This is it, everyone!" the man from the news exclaimed. "We've found our tree!"

But the news crew walked right past tiny Albert to Big Betty, the eighty-foot evergreen behind him.

Albert craned his trunk to see the mighty tree. Next to Betty, he looked like a fallen acorn. His eyes welled up and he felt a lump in his trunk.

Maisie patted her best friend on the branches. "It's okay, Al. Maybe you'll be the Empire City Christmas Tree next year."

But Albert knew his dream was over.

Then Albert noticed Cactus Pete hitching a ride on Betty's truck. He was mangled—and he was mad.

"And here I thought this shrimpo was the Empire City Christmas Tree!" Pete snickered. "Thanks for leading me to the *real* thing. I couldn't have ruined Christmas without ya!"

Albert couldn't let Pete get away with it. With Maisie and Gene at his side, he snuck aboard the news van and headed to New York!

At last, they were there! Empire City Square. The purple sky swirled in the stinging December wind. Maisie's teeth chattered!

A massive crowd gathered around Betty, ready to ring in the season.

Albert, Maisie, and Gene spotted Cactus Pete. He was aiming a spike right at the crane operator who was about to put the famous star on Betty's head.

"Look," Pete cackled.
"A fallin' star!"

POP! WHIZ! SHING! Pete's needles
pierced the operator right in the heinie,
sending the star swinging above. It sliced
Betty's top clean off!

"I'm bald!" Betty cried.

There was no place to put the famous
star! Christmas was ruined.

Albert looked out at the heartbroken crowd.
Right in the middle, he saw Molly, the girl from
the nursery! He remembered what she had told him:
*"It's okay to be small, as long as it doesn't stop you
from doin' big things."*

Albert had an idea! But he needed help. . . .

People in the crowd gave Albert some new decorations, and the crane operator hoisted him up.

And up!

And up.

Cameras flashed and the crowd
cheered as Albert was lifted onto Betty's
peak and the spectacular star was placed
on top of his head. At three feet tall,
he was a perfect fit!

Albert had done it! He had become the most famous
Christmas tree in the world! But when he looked down at
Maisie and Gene waving goodbye, he realized something was
missing: his family at Earth Mama's nursery. Christmastime
just didn't feel like Christmastime without them.

Then Albert saw Cactus Pete. He was sad and alone.
"You don't hate Christmas," Albert said. An idea was
sparking inside him. "You just hate being left out. How'd
you like to be shiny and twinkly for once?"

Albert traded places with the cactus. Pete immediately started singing at the top of his lungs. *"O Cactus Pete! O Cactus Pete! How heavenly are thy needles!"*

Big Betty rolled her eyes. "This is gonna be one long holiday."

Albert, Maisie, and Gene looked at Pete and smiled. It was time to go home.

On Christmas morning, all the plants at Earth Mama's nursery awoke to find Albert, Maisie, and Gene back from their big-city adventure.

"We're so glad you're here!" exclaimed a Venus flytrap named Jaws. "We missed not having a Christmas tree to call our own!"

Molly, Donny, and Earth Mama walked through the door. The tiny girl stuck a tiny star right on Albert's peak.

"Every real Christmas tree needs a star," she said with a smile. When she turned away, Albert smiled back brightly. It was going to be the Christmas-iest Christmas after all.